LIMITLESS

Poetry of an Aromantic & Asexual Journey

PATRICK BEX

First Edition
ISBN: 979-8-9918363-0-2

This is a work of creative nonfiction. These poems reflect true
experiences from the author's life. Names and identifying details
have been omitted to respect the privacy of individuals.

https://www.fluentlyaspec.com

Publisher | Fluently Aspec
Cover design | Mykola Shelepa
Editing and Typesetting | Kexa

But my identity is not brokenness;
it's whatever I choose it to be
I know that person in the mirror now,
and nothing is going to break me.

CONTENTS

To *Kelly-*

You have been with me at every step on
this journey of self-discovery.
A shoulder to lean on,
an open mind to listen and learn,
and a compassionate heart that always
believed in me.

I would not be here without your love and support.

back to no

Sometimes I feel left behind
and I sort of don't get why.
I don't even want those things,
but play along with the lie.
And yet, something pulls at me
when watching others go.
Sometimes I wish to just say "yes,"
But it always comes back to no.

bury

How does everyone know
what it's like to have a crush?
Do I just randomly pick a girl,
or should I wait for one to blush?
When did everyone learn all this?
Did I miss that lesson in class?
There better not be a test for this,
because I don't think I'd pass.

Is it weird that all the dates I have had
were with girls who asked me first?
Is there something here I just don't get,
or have I secretly been cursed?
They keep talking about these butterflies,
and this nervousness I'd feel.
But I only get that for my best friends,
so, I hope to God that's not real.

Because either I can't fall for anyone,
in which case I might be unwell,
or I only fall for my best friends,
the ones I can never tell.
I can't risk hurting what we have,
so, I'll bury my feelings deep below.
Maybe it's true what everyone says -
that when it's romantic love, I'll know.

third wheel

I know it's unintentional,
but I'm always the third wheel —
or the fifth, or seventh,
or ninth, or eleventh,
and I don't always like the way I feel.

I try not to let it bother me,
I brush it off, say it's not a big deal.
I tell myself I'm alright,
but every movie night
is becoming my Achilles' heel.

Don't get me wrong, I love my friends,
but I don't want them to know.
I'm watching myself fall behind;
It's becoming too hard to conceal
that the kind of love they share in pairs
is something I might never feel.

They tell me I'm a late bloomer,
that I'll know when it's real.
But the love I want is for my friends,
the other stuff holds no appeal.
I'm afraid that if I tried explaining,
they'd think it's all a spiel,
or they'd think I'm a loveless freak
with a heart made of steel.

I wish they could understand
that for me, friendship is ideal.
But I'm losing my grip, fading back,
afraid I won't even be a wheel.

lunch period note

I didn't know if it was a date,
but then your hand was in mine.
I wish I could tell you how I was feeling,
but I was still waiting for a sign.
The movie you picked was a comedy,
a satire film about sports.
I thought we were going as friends,
but then I felt out of sorts.

I want to like you; I really do,
but I don't know if love is real.
It's like everyone learned this skill but me.
Why am I unable to feel?

It's been three months since the first date,
and you deserve to have that love returned.
So you broke up with me in a note,
and now it's my lesson learned.
Maybe I'm not cut out to be a boyfriend,
like you suggested in your letter.

I don't know why I am this way,
But I know that you deserve better.

dorm room wall

I've lost track of time —
How long have I been staring
at the decorations on our wall,
and my new roommate's lack of caring?

He didn't ask my opinion
on this wall, both his and mine,
before he taped up still-enclosed "protection"
across from my bed in a peace sign.

It's only week two of college,
but I'm afraid of what's in store.
I used to think it's all in movies;
I don't know what "normal" is anymore.

Someone got caught hooking up
in the lounge just down the hall,
and I can't get a moment's peace
with that peace sign on our wall.

Am I the problem here?
Was there a meeting that I missed?
Everyone else got a different memo —
The most I've done is kissed.

Is there something wrong with me?
I can't relate at all —
Not with the parties or the hookups
or this contradiction on my wall.

vacancy

Is it so wrong to want a night
Without being teased and coerced?
Nothing about this feels all right;
I don't want something if it's forced
My friends insist that I need to "get some,"
And that their mission is to assist.
Am I broken or just plain dumb?
I'm feeling handcuffed at the wrist.

I get that it's what I'm supposed to want
But why do they make it a big deal?
Is intimacy something I'm supposed to flaunt?
Is this actually how people feel?

Is there something the matter with me
if I don't want it like others crave?
Does that part of my brain have a vacancy,
Or am I dead inside, one foot in the grave?

normal

I don't know what normal is anymore.
I thought I knew.
For four years, sure, things were whispered,
but I didn't think it was real.
My friends didn't brag about it;
It wasn't all in my face —
well, aside from movies,
and TV, and magazines, and music.

Wait.
All this time,
they were serious.
I didn't think they were,
but now here I am,
starting college with a random roommate
who tapes condoms to the wall
in a peace sign
and calls it art.

Every
so often,
I notice a lonely piece of tape
where one used to hang,
sometimes replaced with a new one.
Sometimes not.

I don't know what normal is anymore.

found words

So many years
without words,
without knowing,
without access,
without meaning.

Found words,
connected words —
broken,
like so many others,
but never broken.

Invented words—
Self-sexual? No.
Non-sexual? Perhaps.
Accessible words.
Bisexual? Zero equals zero.
What am I?

Back of my mind —
someone said it once
years ago.
What was it?
Asexual?
Is that right?
Is that me?

I don't feel different;
I still feel like me.
But I still can't comprehend
being different.

Everything I thought I knew.
everything I understood,
not like everyone around me.
They really are like in movies and books?
They really think about it this much?
They NEED it?

So many new questions,
so many new fears,
but so much new light —
streams of purple through the clouds.

Community.
Answers.
Found words,
connecting us,
holding the door open
for others to find their words too.

that word

She caught me off guard.
When did our friendship evolve
to physicality?
And shouldn't I want this too?

I think I love her;
I want to love her.
So why don't I feel right about this?
Why don't I want this like she does?

She said I must have it in me;
she said we're sexual beings —
whatever that means.
Unless I'm what?
What was that word?
Asexual.

23

Asexual.
Is that what I am?
Is that why I don't want this?
I stare at my phone,
wondering what to say next

She's done waiting.
Says my mind seems to change too much.
She's gone.

But that word remains:
Asexual.

hoping for strength – *a nonet*

I fear I've lost control of my path.
There is so much that concerns me.
Why can't I love the same way
like other people do?
I still lie awake,
Hoping for strength
To accept
I am
Ace

the realization – *a haiku*

Isolation grows.
Allonormativity —
wherever I go.

pretending

I know
what you want for me —
what you think I
should want for myself,
what you planned for me:
the roadmaps, the hope,
the family picture frame.

I don't know
how to tell you,
to explain to you
what my body wants,
what my heart wants,
and what it rejects —
that I'm not made the same.

I don't know
when will be the right time,
when will be the right place
to show you,
to guide you,
to stop hiding myself,
to free me from this shame.

I don't know
if a place exists,
if a time exists
to see me clearly
without you searching
for someone to blame.

But I know
that for now I'll keep quiet,
keep pretending,
keep smiling and nodding —
though inside
I feel myself rotting,
twisting and turning,
all to keep playing your game.

keep it inside

I don't think I can say it —
I'm scared you won't understand.
Because if what I think is true,
it ruins all you had planned.

We never talked about sex;
you left that to my health teacher,
aside from saying to wait 'til marriage,
or else I'd answer to our preacher.

And every time I tried to tell you,
you'd let me know you'll say a prayer,
in hopes that God will send "the one,"
someone I know isn't there.

I don't want to let you down,
and I know what that takes.
I'll have to keep it all inside
for both of our sakes.

your plans – *a cinquain*

I am
sorry to you
that I cannot fulfill
the plans you made because of who
I am.

enough

Do you think I'm enough?
 I tried to be.
  First, to be enough as a friend,
   but felt they deserved better than me.
   I tried to be enough as a partner,
    but that kind of love never grew.
    I tried to wish it out of thin air,
     so I could be the boyfriend they knew.
     Sometimes it doesn't seem fair,
      the things I want — never to be.

your opinion

Who are you to say
that asexuality is not real?
Where do you get off
saying it's no big deal?
It's not a lack of interest,
or me missing the appeal.
It's not about things I don't like —
it's about what I don't feel.
I'm attracted to no one;
that's just how it is for me.
Attraction works on a spectrum
with countless ways to be.
Just because you don't understand
doesn't make something fake.
So, keep your opinion to yourself —
I didn't ask for your take.

obligation

For many years, I wondered
if the problem was me —
if our short-lived relationship ended
because of my asexuality.

For so long I wondered:
was I not enough for you?
Would I ever really know?
Did I even deserve to?

You made it clear what you wanted,
and I always felt the blame.
Come to think of it, I realize —
you never asked me the same

We never talked about it —
your unspoken expectation.
So, instead, you found somebody else
to fill that obligation.

We broke up four days later,
but I already knew,
because my friends and I saw you that night
and watched him go home with you.

Over the years, my perspective has changed,
and now I clearly see:
the problem was never who I was —
but that you weren't enough for me.

I'm the one who deserved more —
more respect and communication,
because I know now that self-care
is my most important obligation.

I give myself the love and respect
and patience at long last.
Maybe I'll find someone new,
but you?
You can stay there in the past.

often

Often, I'm asked if I'm alone —
if ever thoughts cross my mind
when I have no one of my own
and couples are everywhere I find.

Often, I'm asked if I have regret
for figuring out my identity.
When friends are married but I'm not yet,
is there growing resent in me?

Often, I'm asked, or even accused
of making it all up in my head.
They say, "Our urges are like a fuse,
an insatiable fire to be fed."

Often, I'm told to seek out treatment
because they say something's wrong.
They think I should be in bereavement
for a future already gone.

Often, I hear the not-so-quiet doubts
and feel the judgmental stares.
They say, "You can't know until you try it out!"
and ask why anyone should care.

Often isn't always,
though sometimes it seems
the role my asexuality plays
has stomped on other people's dreams.

Often, I must remind myself
that I decide my own fate.
I must put my pride on the top shelf
and pay no mind to their hate.

Often, I breathe in deep
and close the comments section.
No matter how low they may steep,
I know my life's direction.

Often, I find simple joy in friends,
as close today as we've been.
And while the invalidation never ends,
its effects are wearing thin.

Always, they try to tear me down,
but I'll pursue my best way to live.
Soon, their words will fall without a sound —
because I've zero effs to give.

trust

I finally found the word for me
that explains my lack of lust —
a way to describe myself,
and why sex is not a must.

Why the very idea of it
fills me with disgust,
in every conversation on sex
into which I'm thrust.

But how do I talk about it?
Who can I trust
when asexuality is treated
as if it's a myth to bust?

time

It's time to let go
of the anger and the guilt.
It's time that you know
this is just how you were built.

It's time for you to hear
that you are not incomplete.
You no longer need to fear
if something's wrong with your heartbeat.

It's time for you to see
that you are never alone,
that asexuality
can be a word that feels like home.

Let the hurt wash away
the moment you hear it spoken,
and remind yourself each day:
you, my friend, were never broken.

asexual pride

I'll never forget that moment
when I found out there's a phrase —
one that replaced the loneliness
that I thought was just a phase.

I'd heard that term before,
but it was explained all wrong —
not in a way that made sense,
though it was me all along.

It took another five years
to open my eyes and see
that what I misunderstood
really did describe me.

My journey took longer than most,
but I'm grateful for the ride —

> *finding my truth,*
> *myself,*
> *my community,*
> *and my own asexual pride.*

deep breath

Today's the day.
Today, I say it out loud.

I finally tell someone
something I thought, for so long,
was a defect —
a brokenness,
something I thought no one
would ever understand.

But I have to say it.
I have to break free of that brokenness,
of that power
it holds over me.

I've practiced what I'd say
over and over
and over,
staring back in the mirror.

But that mirror is back at home,
and I am here —
and she's walking toward me,
sitting down across from me.

A friend.

Over a decade of memories,
over a decade of talks.
And though none of those talks
were quite like this —
I know.

I know she will still see me.

Deep breath.
And I share my truth.

your brother

I walked in, unsure what to say,
afraid I wouldn't make any sense.
I sat there, trying to wish it away,
my entire body feeling so tense.

> I wanted to make the hurt inside
> finally meet its end,
> but there I sat, so terrified
> to come out to an old friend.

> But you looked at me with an open heart,
> and knew something was on my mind.
> I took a deep breath to start,
> and seized the words I struggled to find.

I was afraid if you knew I was ace,
your friendly gaze would harden.
But instead, a smile crossed your face,
and it lit up the entire garden.

You told me you were proud of me,
that you knew what I'd said was tough.
You promised that one day I'd see
that the love I feel is enough.

Today, I'm still so glad it was you
I told before any other.
We started as friends,
but for all we've been through,
you are my sister,
and I'll always be your brother.

wrapped – *a haiku*

Arms securely wrapped,
the warm embrace of a friend
assuring I'm loved.

unequivocally

You have always been there for me;
I know I can always depend
on you to listen, to learn with me —
I've never had to pretend.

You understand I don't get those feelings;
there'll be no wedding to attend.
You've never judged or criticized
all the time I choose to spend
chasing dreams instead of dates,
or all the choices you recommend.

Yet, when my heart was broken still,
you were always there to mend.
You've been there for me from day one,
and I know you will be to the end.

If I need a shoulder to cry on,
yours is always there to lend.
I don't know where I'd be without you —

you are unequivocally,
undoubtedly,
my best friend.

dating profile

I put *asexual* in my dating profile
because it's important to me that they know.
I put asexual in my dating profile —
but that doesn't mean I want to take things slow.

I put *asexual* in my dating profile,
yet they still ask if I want to give it a go.
I put asexual in my dating profile,
hoping they'd understand that no means no.

But still, they ask invasive questions
or suggest that I need medication.
Some mock me, call me immature,
Or push the priesthood as my vocation.

Google is free; it's not my job
to teach or debunk all this misinformation.
And when they get short with me,
they can't clearly see —
we're both feeling two kinds of frustration.

Still, they send me photos,
hoping I'll feel some sensation.
It's sad, really — I liked their personality,
but I'll block them for this attempt at temptation.

So, I took down
my dating profile.
I don't need
the invalidation.

not you

I know that you're mad,
I didn't say it to you.
I know this sounds bad,
but I don't know what to do.
I look in the mirror,
and question what's wrong —
why I can't repeat what I hear
in every love song.

But I keep trying,
keep lying,
keep pulling and prying,
keep vying —
then crying,
and back to denying.

Why can't I feel
like they do in the books?
Is love even real,
or is it all just for looks?
I need time away
to not feel empty.
It's true, but hard to say…

It's not you, it's me.

i think, maybe...

"So good,
it kind of made me cry."
"What book?" she asks.
"It's called Loveless," I reply,
digging it out of my bag,
placing it in her hand.
And I think—
maybe I should tell her.
Maybe she'll understand.

"Can I
ask you something?"
She nods, and I
fumble through my phrasing.
"When we were... us...
was I romantic?
I know I'm not the other thing."
Her stare makes me frantic.

"Yes," she says,
"like on Valentine's Day
and our six-month anniversary.
Why do you ask?"

"This book—
it talks the way my brain talks.
I think maybe…
maybe I'm aromantic.
I want to learn if it's me."

She nods,
softly smiling,
a light toss of her hair.
"Well," she says,
"we can learn together,
'cause I'm not going anywhere."

52

another journey – *a haiku*

Another journey —
ripping my sense of self down.
My heart beats for none.

no sailboat

Romance feels like an optical illusion,
hidden somewhere within a canvas.
But as I stare, it builds confusion
in every shape I try to look past.

They tell me it's at the center,
that if I relax, I'll clearly see.
But it remains an unsolved riddle
why love seems nowhere near me.

In those pictures, their twisting motions,
I see no dog, no horse, no sailboat,
no vision across the swirling ocean;
if love is an island, mine's remote.

do you know?

Do you know what it's like?
To spend years in the dark
and watch while loves spreads like fire,
but you've never felt a spark.

Do you know how it feels?
To be told that you're wrong,
that the words you found are made up,
when you know it's where you belong.

Do you know the sting of being told?
"You just haven't found them yet,"
and you listen,
and you try,
and you try some more,
but no closer can you get.

Have you seen the hope in someone's eyes
quickly turn to panic,
as they realize their plans for you were wrong?

I have.
I'm aromantic.

my phone remains silent

"But I love you too,
and I don't want to lose it,"
is what my heart wants to say,
but my mouth will refuse it.
I know it's not fair
to stand in my friends' way,
though I'm scared they'll drift further
until they forget me one day.

Everyone else is falling in love,
but I feel like I'm just standing still,
and I wish they could see that my love is just as strong,
but I'm afraid that they never will.

Though my love is different,
my intentions unique,
my heart beats just like theirs,
and I don't want to lose them,
but my phone remains silent.

I wonder which of them cares...

taco bell parking lot

Why am I like this?
What did I do?
I don't relate to my friends anymore —
the ones I grew up with,
listening to Fall Out Boy
on the hoods of our cars
in the Taco Bell parking lot
at 1:30 AM.

But that was almost 20 years ago.
We aren't kids anymore.
They have their own —
their own kids,
their own marriages,
their own lives.

That parking lot, where we asked
such essential life questions:
Where would we be?
What should we do?
Will we fall in love?

Those questions are now answered,
but I still feel like
I never left that parking lot.

did i waste her time?

Did I waste her time?
Was I fair to her?
Every moment her hand was in mine
all feels like a blur.

I know now how our love was different
and our wants didn't align.
I understand what she really meant
when she told me things were fine.

I didn't know there were words for this;
I hadn't found them yet.
I didn't realize the things I'd miss
or the attractions I didn't get.

When I couldn't feel that storybook bliss,
it would have been nice, I bet.
Still, I wouldn't trade one single kiss —
she's still the best I've ever met.

what others want for me

I do not hate romance;
I enjoy watching from the outside.
Seeing those I care about happy
fills my own heart with pride.

I do not hate weddings —
three times I've been best man.
There's nothing like seeing that journey
and knowing where my friends began.

Sure, there are moments that can be hard;
sometimes, I have to leave the room,
because I can't give those moments to others,
and I might never be a groom.

I might not dance with my mother
or give my sisters a new sister to embrace.
I know they'd never be upset with me,
but I'm scared to admit this to their face.

Being aromantic isn't hard for me,
but what's hard is not wanting what others do.
I still sometimes worry what others want for me —
does that ever get easier too?

rankings

Something's been bothering me, I want to confess.
We downplay friendship, like somehow, it's less —
like we never depend on friends when in a mess,
like they aren't there to ease our stress.

As if they don't cheer on each victory,
as if they aren't part of our story.
Why do we make it seem mandatory
to rank friendship in a lesser category?

Why do relationships need a label?
As if words make them somehow more stable,
or elevate them to a mythical fable.
So I say right now, we lay it all on the table.

Romance isn't "more", it runs a parallel line,
and labels are just words you assign.
If romance isn't for you, that's perfectly fine —
cherish your friendships, like I cherish mine.

devoid

People think I'm devoid of love
because I'm aroace.
They think I'm hollow inside,
but that's just not the case.

They don't know where my head was at
before I figured it out.
They don't know the brokenness I felt,
or the anger and self-doubt.

It took time, but once I knew,
I started to feel something strange —
the brokenness began slipping away,
and in my heart, I felt a change.

They think I'm devoid of love
because it's not how they want it to be.
But I love family, friends, and community,
and for the first time in a long time, I love me.

tried

I tried —
I tried to let romance in.
I tried to be the boyfriend,
to be the partner.
I tried to feel.
I tried to live in the moment,
to take it all in.
The snowflakes in your hair,
the light in your eyes,
from my friend's white Suburban
stalled in that high school parking lot,
waiting for us to get in the backseat —
you waiting for me,
waiting for our first kiss.

I tried to believe you,
there in that backseat,
when you played the new ringtone
you put on your phone,
so every time I called,
you'd hear "Stolen" by Dashboard Confessional.
You told me you chose it
because that's what I'd done to your heart.

I tried, for you.
But I was 17,
it was 2007,
and I didn't have the right words yet.
The word aromantic had only been online
for two years by then —
it wouldn't reach me for another decade.

I still believe we could've been good friends,
maybe even to this day.
And I still think about you;
I hope you found the love you were looking for.

I'm still trying to find what love means for me.
But I know in my heart,
I'm grateful for the time we had —
I'm grateful that we tried.

specter

When you say you love me like a friend,
could you please stop starting with "only"?
Because I know you already tend
to look at me like I'm lonely.

Stop looking at my life
and thinking it's dreary.
Stop hoping that I'll find a wife —
just listen, and please hear me.

You're right — it's not what we envisioned
when we were only ten years old.
But my love life is not your mission,
just let my story unfold.

Please listen, because I love you too,
and to me, friendship means the most.
But when you say, "I miss the old you,"
you make me feel like I'm a ghost.

I'm proud to be aroace —
I'm not a specter you see through.
If you can't give me that respect and grace,
then maybe this friendship needs review.

aspec happiness

What is happiness?
Because apparently, I'm doing it wrong.
Why can't happiness be
singing along to my favorite song?

Why can't it be driving alone,
under the starry skies,
or watching the sun set on the lake,
the air alive with fireflies?

Why can't happiness mean
embracing the relationships I've found?
Why must I need a romantic partner
when I've got the best people around?

Why do others decide
what my happiness should be?
No one else controls my voice—
my joy comes from being me.

They don't like that I'm aromantic,
and they don't like that I'm ace,
but as long as I'm me, I'm happy.
They'll never wipe the smile off my face.

the vents

I feel like I can finally breathe,
 like the vents are finally opened,
  and light seeps through the window at last,
   touching my face like an old friend.
    For years, I breathed in toxic air,
     coughing through the pollution,
      as year after year, I was fed the lie
       that marriage and sex were life's conclusion.
        But never again will someone tell me,
         "Don't give up! You'll find her one day!"
          No one can say I'm too young to understand,
           because I see right through what they say.
            I won't concede that my script's been written —
             I'm writing it on my own.
              And for those who fear that I'm lonely?
               They can simply leave me alone.

grief

When I learned my identity,
 I expected to feel grief —
  like I'd lost a whole part of me,
   that was my belief.
    It felt like it had been ripped away
     by some menacing thief,
      but now I've got to say,
       it's such a huge relief.
        I'm over dating, hidden glances,
         questions so impersonal and brief.
          I'm done with the awkward dances,
           done with the whole worn-out motif.
            I'm my own best date, I'll say it loud.
            I'll turn over a new leaf.
            I am aromantic, I am proud
            and I don't need your grief.

break

I don't need permission to be myself —
my approval comes from my heart.
Those who have a problem with who I am
never really knew me from the start.

I don't need to listen to those
who still refuse to hear me.
I know myself better than anyone;
I know things they'll never see.

I'm aromantic, I'm asexual —
things some refuse to comprehend.
They try to harass and argue with me,
but I won't break or bend.

I won't be silenced from speaking my truth
because I remember the fear,
how it feels to be without those words —
a broken stranger in the mirror.

But my identity is not brokenness;
it's whatever I choose it to be
I know that person in the mirror now,
and nothing is going to break me.

still no sailboat

I'm still staring, years later,
at the image in front of me.
Though older now, the chase continues,
and I admit, begrudgingly,
that I still can't see that sailboat —
some things just aren't meant to be.
I've aged, but my story hasn't changed.
Some days I wish that wasn't me.

starry skies

I see in ways that escape most eyes,
a quiet ability of mine.
When I gaze into the starry skies,
I see life's fragility shine.

In each star, I see my friends —
each one glowing like the last.
I see a love that never ends,
as strong as days long past.

I don't fixate on romance stories
or desire a physical touch.
I focus on the love before me
and let society adjust.

move along

I am not always strong —
I've just gotten better at faking.
I am not always sure
of the paths I'm taking.

I am not so together,
just barely avoiding breaking.
But I'll push on,
no matter how much I'm aching.

I keep moving my feet,
even as the pain is caking.
With every step I take,
I can feel that pain flaking.

And though I'm scared to admit,
with a voice that's still shaking —
I'm a work in progress,
a masterpiece in the making.

forward

Another year gone by,
and this one really flew —
a chance to look back
on all the ways I've come through.

I wish I could say
I've stepped more into my own,
or that I have let go
of the fear of ending up alone.

But I'm a work in progress,
one step, day by day.
The good moments grow,
and the bad fades away.

Acceptance was tough,
embrace isn't always eventual.
But I'll keep moving forward
with pride as an asexual.

What matters is knowing
I'm better now than before.
This next year, I'll keep growing,
looking ahead to what's in store.

one name

Just because it has one name
 does not make all love the same.
  I once tried to play that game,
   but in time, resentment came.
    I stared in the mirror, feeling nothing but shame —
     angry and hurt, and only me to blame.
      But the picture was too small,
       I needed a bigger frame.
        To find my own kind of love,
         to burn my own flame,
          to cast a wider net
           and widen the scope of my aim.
            Now I see myself, my aroace self,
             and I can break free from the claim
              that what every human wants
               is to love the same.

spoilers

It's not that I miss her —
 how can I?
  We've never met.
   And I can't miss a feeling
    if I've never felt it yet.
     So, what am I looking for?
      What is it that I'm after?
       I'm not looking for my future bride,
        just someone to share in laughter.
         I'm not chasing a romance story,
          but a story all my own,
           with its own plot and resolution,
            and a unique mood and tone.
             I've always walked a different path,
              and romance isn't for me.
               The only thing I avoid is spoilers
                to my aromantic love story.

an adjacent road

They say it's better to have loved and lost
than to never have loved at all,
but those who say that don't know the cost
of feelings hidden behind a wall.

Some days, I wish I'd known quicker,
I wonder how life would be.
It sounds nice, but here's the kicker—
would I even still be me?

If I had walked an adjacent road
or even jogged a faster pace,
or had to carry a different load,
would I have found that I'm aroace?

Would I have found this community—
these strong, encouraging souls,
if I hadn't had that journey in me
and had to pay those highway tolls?

Still, it took some more roads traveled
to learn that love is what we make it to be.
And on this journey, one more love unraveled,
I finally learned to love me for me.

reconstruction

I'm done wanting something different.
I'm over wishing I could change.
I'm sick of hoping I'd grow out of it
or that my feelings would rearrange.
Being aroace made me feel alone,
but a friend taught me how to reframe,
to reconstruct my way of thinking,
and I've never been the same.

I no longer think I'm missing out
if it's not the right fit for me.
I'm not losing those relationships;
I have brighter ones to see.
All those things I thought about myself
were just born from insecurity,
but now I know I was never broken,
I was on my path to self-discovery.

I used to let others get inside my head,
that I was running out of time.
But I have my friends, my family, and myself,
so this aroace is thriving in his prime.

limitless

My love is not limited,
it knows no restraint or bounds.
I feel love for my closest friends,
for family, both blood and found.

For the gentle rain on an April day,
the sun setting behind the trees,
the light reflecting off the lake,
and the subtlest hint of a breeze.

I love to write; I love to sing;
I love the pounding in my chest,
the vibrations pumping through the ground
at a summer music fest.

I know others see me alone,
and they think, "What a shame."
But I'm aroace, and I love myself,
and love has more than just one name.

roads

I grew up thinking
there was only one road,
and I could barely move,
carrying that load.

Weighed down to the floor
by immense expectations,
I could never find love;
all I found was frustration.

I couldn't tell anyone
because if those words were spoken,
they'd say that it's made up
or tell me that I'm broken.

But it really does exist,
though I never knew the word.
It's called aromantic,
and I felt whole when I heard.

I learned we all have journeys,
roads both parallel and intersecting,
that I can still love myself,
the one I've been neglecting.

I can love my friends
and follow a path that's right for me.
I've learned to break expectations
with this newfound community.

holiday questions

Give yourself permission
to feel what's inside.
I've been asked those questions,
and many times, I've lied.

You don't need to run from it,
and you don't need to hide.
When asked if I have a girlfriend
I'd tell them that I've tried.

When asked when I'll get married,
I brushed those questions aside.
They don't know how it feels
or how many times I've cried.

When I didn't know the reason
and had no one to confide,
that I didn't want to have kids
and I'm not looking for a bride.

You don't have to answer;
you can just let it slide.
You know what's in your heart —
let the truth be your guide.
I know I'm not alone in this,
the identity I once denied.
I'm aromantic asexual,
a spectrum deep and wide.

I don't let those questions bother me;
I'll ignore them now in stride.
And this year when I celebrate,
I'll do so with aroace pride.

not a phase

At five years old when I played superheroes,
they never fought the bad guys.
I'd take my Tommy and my Kimberly,
and they'd stare into each other's eyes.

At ten years old when I watched TV,
I tried to laugh along,
but all the sex jokes on TGIF
just sounded wrong.

At twelve in my Catholic school,
I learned the birds and the bees,
We were told to sign a celibate contract.
I thought, "They think that's hard? Please!"

At fifteen years old I played my part
in the boys' locker room.
I told myself it'd all work out,
I'm still just yet to bloom.

At eighteen years old I went off to school
and learned I was far behind,
with a roommate who taped condoms to our wall
and never asked if I'd mind.

At twenty-one I had a girlfriend.
She said she'd wait, but that was a lie.
Her friends would constantly message me,
and I'd find her with another guy.

At twenty-three my so-called friend
convinced himself to help me out,
but all he did was fill my head
with hopelessness and self-doubt.

At twenty-five I forced myself,
convinced I needed to get it done.
With my virginity, I lost myself
and felt more like an aberration.

I shut it down, closed it off,
and put it all out of mind.
For the next three years, my thoughts would spiral —
unforgiving, unrelenting, and unkind.

At twenty-eight in the Phoenix night,
I finally found the phrase.
I learned I'd always been asexual,
that for me, it's not a phase.

So, for all the years I have left,
I will shout it for all to see,
just in case there's someone out there
on that same journey as me.

many shapes – *a haiku*

Love takes many shapes.
My heart beats for my best friends,
they are my comfort.

dear me, from me

Dear 13, you don't have to kiss her.
Dear 16, it's okay to cry.
Dear 19, she'll understand.
You don't have to lie.
Dear 21, what she did was wrong,
So forgive yourself today.
Dear 26, don't let this one go;
You'll love her another way.
Dear 28, you're almost there;
You've finally found your place.
By 32, you'll love being you —
Unbreakable aroace.

my sailboat

I realized something about the sailboat.
The ways I love are too much to quantify.
All those people focus on that one boat
because it's the first thing to catch their eye.

Maybe I should shift my focus
and see the bigger picture behind the glass —
the details others take for granted,
the other things they look right past.

Maybe I focus too much on what I want
that I forget to focus on what's around.
I can't see that one sailboat they're after,
but I can love the sailboats I have found.

my plans – *a cinquain*

I am
making new plans,
moving away from yours,
drawing new paths reflecting who
I am

to all the girls

To all the girls I've loved before,
I'm sorry it wasn't the love you wanted,
and I'm sorry I couldn't say the words
that all the other couples flaunted.
I'm sorry for how I left things,
with all the questions still burning.
I'm sorry you never really knew me —
it's a journey, and I'm still learning.

There's a reason I would pull away,
a reason I seemed so frantic.
I only recently found the word.
It turns out I'm aromantic.

We both deserve happiness,
to find whatever we're after.
You might not have been my story's end,
but I'm forever grateful for our chapter.

forgiveness

I know that you didn't understand,
and I'm not mad anymore.
You thought you were doing what's best for me,
but you didn't know me at my core.
You saw what everyone had around us
and thought maybe I was broken.
You tried to force that onto me,
but were afraid and left the truth unspoken.

I forgive you for hurting me,
for leaving me in the dark,
for every forced attempt, every denial,
for every scar and every mark.
What matters now is we're on the same page,
and you know now that I'm aroace.
As you look back through this mirror,
you see this has always been the case.

I forgive you, the part of me —
the denier I was then
Because we've made it here together now,
and we can learn to love again.

shelf back

My story is still unfolding,
and I don't know how it will end.
I don't know how the binding is molding,
or how the shelf back might bend.

Not sure if the wording will feel pedantic,
but I do know my character traits.
Fearless, asexual, kind, aromantic,
patiently looking to whatever awaits.

I'm unsure of the cover when the copy is bound,
or what title will grace the spine.
But within these pages, love will be found
uniquely, asexually, aromantically, mine.

Passion and humor will fill each sentence,
tales of adventure with family and friend.
I'll breathe in every word still in present tense,
because I'm still writing how it will end.

more

Growing up I never heard
of asexuality before,
but learning about it
became a mandatory chore,
because I always knew
I was different at my core —
different from other guys
who bragged about their score.
As the years went on,
I couldn't ignore
the questions I held
lurking behind the door.

But where are the answers?
There's so little rep to look for.
I can't just turn on the TV
or walk into a bookstore.

Sure, some exist,
but we deserve so much more.
We deserve our own stories,
and we demand more diverse lore.

For every ace person
to find the answers they look for,
the stories to connect to,
and the experiences to explore.

We need more diverse voices
given a chance to soar.
You've heard my voice;
I want to hear yours.

Publication History

The following poems have previously been posted
on the Fluently Aspec social media accounts on
TikTok, Instagram, and YouTube:

"dear me; from me", "starry skies", "often",
"did i waste her time?", "limitless", "forgiveness",
 "out loud", "break", "what others want from
me", "devoid", "time", "more", "tried", "do you
know?", "i think, maybe…", "holiday questions",
"grief", "my phone remains silent", "spoilers",
"roads", "specter", "dating profile",
"aspec happiness", "not you;", "dorm room wall",
"lunch period note",
"to all the girls", "your brother", "shelf back",
"an adjacent road", "Asexual pride", "forward",
"reconstruction", "third wheel", and "rankings."

"one name" was previously featured in AZE
Journal in volume 6, issue 4.

Additional Resources on the Aromantic and Asexual Spectrums

AVEN (Asexuality Visibility & Education Network):
- http://www.asexuality.org
- Instagram/Threads: @aven.pt

AUREA (The Aromantic-spectrum Union for Recognition, Education, and Advocacy):
- https://aromanticism.org
- Instagram/Threads: @aurea_aromantic

TAAAP (The Ace and Aro Advocacy Project):
- https://www.taaap.org
- Instagram/Threads: @theaceandaroadvocacyproject

The Asexual Agenda:
- https://www.asexualagenda.wordpress.com

Asexuality Archive:
- https://www.asexualityarchive.com

Acknowledgements

To my family - I know what I believe and who I am, and a lot of that comes from you.

To Chaz, Justin, Steph, Amanda, Melissa, and Ben - You have been the most loyal friends I could have ever asked for— caring, curious, and willing to learn. You are some of my oldest companions, knowing me long before I knew the words in this book. You were with me in classrooms, on school buses, and at dances as I felt myself falling behind, not understanding why. Even when I was hard on myself, I always knew I could count on you.

To Jessiye - Thank you for creating a space where I first learned to open up about my experiences. Without the support group you welcomed me into with open arms, I might not have found the confidence to go from speaking to a few people on those Google Meets to sharing openly on the internet. You gave me the courage to put myself out there, and I'm forever grateful for that.

To Sophie - Thank you for being such an inspiration in my writing and for your guidance on turning this dream into reality. This book would not exist without you.

To Cody - Thank you for teaching me, believing in me, and helping me learn to believe in myself.

To Rachel, Alyshia, and Lynn - Thank you for showing me that my voice matters and that sharing my truths can help others find their own.

About the Author

Patrick Bex (he/him; real name Patrick Bergen) is an aromantic and asexual poet, content creator, educator, and advocate known by his social media handle Fluently Aspec. In addition to his writing and content creation, Patrick has also been involved in promoting aromantic and asexual awareness and education, most notably in his home state of Wisconsin. In 2022, he successfully petitioned for the state's first proclamation of Ace Week, making Wisconsin the eighth state to recognize this event.

To follow Patrick's work and to learn more,
visit https://www.fluentlyaspec.com

For business inquiries, contact fluentlyaspec@gmail.com